This book belongs to:

Just Believe!

Pm

THE Magic Gingerbread House

P. M. Franks
Illustrations by **MIKE GUILLORY**

bright sky press
HOUSTON, TEXAS

"WAKE UP, MOLLIE!" I said. "Mom is starting without us!"

We didn't stop to brush our teeth or comb our hair. We ran downstairs, too excited to waste another minute.

"Good morning, girls!" Mom said. "You're going to make your very own gingerbread house! It will take two days, but it will be beautiful and—if you are lucky—magical. After working hard in Santa's workshop, the elves need a place to relax. If they like our house, they might move in."

"How?" I asked.

"Just believe in the magic of Christmas, and wait and see," Mom told me.

We mixed the dough, rolled it and used stencils to cut the pieces.

"Don't forget the chimney, the front door and the shutters," Mom told us. "It needs to be a special house. Tomorrow, after the pieces harden, we'll build it."

After breakfast the next morning, I poured a little water into a bowl of powdered sugar and Mollie stirred.

"This mortar will hold the house together," Mom told us.

Mollie took a small lick. "Yummy!"

"Save that for the house," Mom said.

We put the pieces together carefully and used the sweet glue and crystal glasses to hold the house together as it dried.

Dad opened a small tin box. "These will bring your gingerbread house to life," he said. I chose a group of children, a miniature Christmas tree, a few presents, and a tiny cat. Mollie picked out a group of carolers, some ice skaters, and seven reindeer. Mom showed us how to spread the snow on the house and cover the yard, and we put the people in place.

"Leave room for ice-skating," said Mom. "The elves really like to play."

Dad turned off the kitchen lights. Our very first gingerbread house lit up inside and out.

"The elves are sure to come tonight!" I said.

Mollie nodded. "I can't wait to see them!"

That night it was hard to get to sleep. We had a hundred questions. Would the elves come live in our gingerbread house? Was it pretty enough? What were they like?

The next morning, we raced down the stairs. The gingerbread house looked exactly the same. "They didn't choose us!" My eyes filled with tears.

"Look, a quarter! And a note!" said Mollie, "Read it!"

Dear Meghan and Mollie,

You made the most beautiful gingerbread house we have ever seen! We are looking forward to spending the Holidays with you. We arrived late last night, so we did not have time to play at the ice skating rink. Hans was disappointed, but we are excited to come back tomorrow night. Have a great day at school. Here is a quarter for rent money.

Love, Your Elves,
Hans, Grietal, Stefan, Kirsten, and Franz

I picked up the quarter. "It's real," I whispered. "Look Mollie! These little footprints weren't here last night." We looked so hard at the house, we didn't even notice Mom getting our lunches packed.

"Hurry up, now, and get ready for school," she said.

"Look, Mommy," said Mollie. "The elves did come last night! They left us rent money with a note. The house *is* magical! But where are they now?"

"My guess is they went back to the North Pole to help Santa get ready," Mom replied. "The elves have work during the day. Just like we do."

"Somebody has to help Santa make all of the toys!" said Dad. "It's the busiest time of year at the North Pole. I'm sure they rush back bright and early to help."

Dear Mollie and Meghan,

We had so much fun tonight! We were tired from working with Santa all day, but we needed some playtime. We ice-skated and roasted marshmallows. We have to leave very early for the North Pole, so I must sleep now. Here is an Advent Calendar to count down the days till Christmas. Be good and study hard.

Love,
Hans

The next morning, we ran as fast as we could down to the kitchen and found their reply.

The next morning when we came into the kitchen, there was another note. We had so many questions, we wrote them right back.

Dear, Elfs
Thank u for r gifts. How is Santa? Do you like the North Pole? How do you get there? We love you. Have you seen a present for us?
Love, Mollie and Meghan
PS Please remind santa we would love a puppy for chrismas

Dear Meghan and Mollie,

We love you too! We are working hard, but we are still having fun. We have seen one gift for Mollie. I know she will love it. We have magic powers so we are able to travel quickly between the North Pole and your gingerbread house. We are so happy to relax here after work. I hope you like your Christmas tree. I love glitter and tinsel!

Love,
Kirsten

We had to practice for the Christmas concert that afternoon. After dinner, Dad set up the little tree between our beds. Mom turned off the lights, and it twinkled in the darkness.

"You girls sure are lucky to have such great elves," said Mom.

Drifting to sleep, we whispered about the elves. Mollie said that they were ice-skating and throwing snowballs. I told her Grietal was nestled by the fire reading.

"Jingle Bells" blasting through the house jolted us awake.

Dad and Mom dashed in. "What are you doing? It's way too late for music!"

"It wasn't us!" I said. "It woke us up too!"

Mom headed downstairs with a baseball bat. Dad followed with a flashlight. We peered down the stairs, but it was too dark to see.

"It was the stereo," Dad said when he came up. "I'm not sure how it started."

"Back to sleep," said Mom. "You don't want to be tired for your concert."

Dear Meghan and Mollie,

I hope that we did not wake you last night. The carolers got everyone in the spirit. I even got Franz to sing a little bit. I didn't realize how loud the CD player would be. We had to get back in the house quickly when your parents came downstairs. Franz was so mad at me for waking everyone up! Sing loudly and smile tonight at your concert. We are going to try to get off work early so we can watch.

Love, Stefan

"I knew it!" I said to Mollie when we read their note the next morning.

We chattered about the elves as Mom fixed our hair. Santa was watching, so we didn't even complain when she curled it.

At the concert, my class waited backstage while Mollie's kindergarten class sang. Next to Mollie, I saw a small girl I had never seen. She barely moved her mouth. This was the best time of the year, but she just looked sad. What could be wrong?

On the way home, I asked Mollie, "Who was that girl with the big brown eyes standing next to you?"

"That's Sammy. She just moved here from Texas at Thanksgiving," Mollie said. "She's quiet."

"She must be lonely," I said.

The next morning, we found ornaments from the elves. After we read their note, I asked Mom if we could have Sammy over.

"Of course," Mom said. "I'll find out how to get in touch with her parents."

Mom discovered that Sammy's parents were in the Army, and they had been called to duty. She was an only child, and she had come to live with her grandparents.

Mom arranged for her to spend the night on Friday. We could make cookies, watch a Christmas movie and try to cheer Sammy up.

"Mollie, we need to be Sammy's friends. Her parents are so far away, and she's in a new place with no friends. She doesn't even have a sister."

"I would be so sad without you, Megs," said Mollie. "We'll always be best friends."

"And, we have the elves," I said.

Dear Mollie and Meghan,

Your concert was wonderful! You sang like angels. We were all so proud of you! We heard you talking about a new girl at school. Maybe you can invite her over to share in the magic of Christmas with you?

Love, Grietal

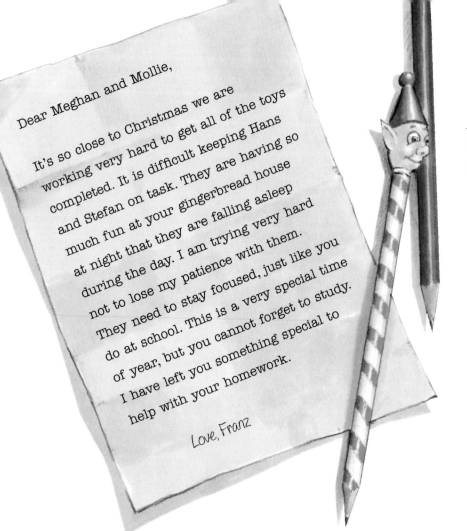

Dear Meghan and Mollie,

It's so close to Christmas we are working very hard to get all of the toys completed. It is difficult keeping Hans and Stefan on task. They are having so much fun at your gingerbread house at night that they are falling asleep during the day. I am trying very hard not to lose my patience with them. They need to stay focused, just like you do at school. This is a very special time of year, but you cannot forget to study. I have left you something special to help with your homework.

Love, Franz

Another note came in the morning, and Sammy's grandparents dropped her off at dinner time. Sammy told us her parents had been stationed at Fort Hood in Texas, but the Army sent them to the Middle East.

"Where is that?" asked Mollie. Dad went into the family room and got our globe. He pointed to the other side of the world. Her mom and dad were very, very far away.

When we showed Sammy the gingerbread house after dinner, she said, "Can you eat it?"

"We could," I said, "But we don't want to. Elves come live in it. They play, sing and give us presents."

"You're making this up!" said Sammy. "I don't like it."

"No, really," Mollie said. We showed her the notes.

"I still don't believe it," said Sammy. Dad turned off the kitchen lights and lit up the gingerbread house. For a minute, her big brown eyes looked almost happy. Then she crossed her arms. "This is stupid."

"Why don't you write a note to them?" Mom said.

"I don't know," she said.

Then she looked at Mom. "Will you help me write it?"

"Tell Meghan what you want to say, and she can write it," said Mom. When we finished, Mom had her sign it.

Dear Elfs,

My name is Sammy. I just moved here from TX. My parents are in the Army and have been deployed to the Middle East. I miss them so much. If you can go to the North Pole can you go to Kuwait and make sure my mommy and daddy are ok. All I want for Christmas is for them to come home.

Love, Sammy

The next morning, we found Sammy standing by the gingerbread house with her mouth open. In her hand was a snow globe.

"It's my mom and dad!" she whispered.

How did the elves know Sammy's parents?

Where did they get the globe?

Dear Sammy,

We are so proud of your parents for serving their country. We know how hard it is for you to be away from them. You are a brave little girl, and we know that Santa has a special present for you on Christmas. Whenever you are lonely or sad, you can look at this snow globe and know that your mom and dad are thinking of you, too. Just believe that they will return safely, and believe in our magic for you.

Love, Stefan, Hans, Kirsten, Grietal and Franz

Little presents and notes continued to arrive. Grietal worked on a rocking horse. Hans kept busy playing tricks on the others, and Franz got frustrated with the mess at the North Pole. Kirsten left us pretty little hair ribbons and fancy rings, and sometimes there would be a new decoration for the gingerbread house. Nothing as mysterious as Sammy's globe appeared again.

Four days before Christmas Eve, Sammy said, "I just want my mom and dad to come home." She started to cry, and we did too. Then she stopped. "Enough sadness! I promised I would be brave, like Mom and Dad are." She wiped her tears with the back of her hand. "Let's write the elves a note!"

Dear Elfs,
We wrote to Santa in July. We really, really, really want a puppy. We promise to take very good care of it. Please, please, please, remind him. Love Megs and Molls.

This is Sammy here. There is nothing I want except my parents. Please tell Santa he dose not need to stop by our house. I don't think anything can make us feel better this year.

Their reply the next morning did not have good news.

Dear Sammy,

We cannot bring your parents home to you until they are finished with their job. As much as they would like to see you, they cannot leave such an important job unfinished. We know how hard this is for you, but just believe in the magic of Christmas, and good things will come to you. We are sure of that. Now, Meghan and Mollie, you know how Santa feels about giving puppies for Christmas. You think that you are ready, but it is more responsibility than you can imagine. Think of something else that you would like, and enjoy your vacation from school.

Love Always, Your Elves

The next morning was cold and rainy. After reading the news about the puppy, Mollie and I poked at breakfast.

Then I had an idea. "Let's make the elves ornaments for their tree!"

"Please, Mom take us to the art store," we begged. "We could pick up Sammy on the way."

"OK," Mom said. "Just give me time to call her grandmother and wrap some presents."

While Mom wrapped, we planned. "Kirsten loves tinsel and glitter," I said. "And we can put some musical notes on the tree for Stefan."

"And little rocking horses for Grietal?" Mollie asked.

I agreed. "And something funny for Hans. But I have no idea for Franz."

We bought colored paper, glitter, crayons, glue, pipe cleaners, tinsel and beads. All that rainy afternoon we made ornaments. Dad added a string of tiny little lights, and the tree was perfect.

"The elves will love it," Mom said.

I realized I hadn't thought about my gift from Santa all day.

Dear Meghan, Mollie
(and Sammy if she is there)

We love ornaments. You thought of something for each of us. Music for Stefan, a rocking horse for Grietal, lots of tinsel for Kirsten, a clown for Hans, and a notebook for me. Thank you! We're off to bed now to get some rest. The next 48 hours are critical. We have left you some reindeer food for Christmas Eve. Dancer and Prancer get really hungry!

All our love,
Your Elves

Mollie looked sadly at me. "I'm going to miss them so much."

I nodded. "They've become a part of our family."

When Christmas Eve arrived, all I could think about was that the elves had gone. I didn't even want to read the note that morning.

Dear Meghan, Mollie and Sammy,

While we are very sad to leave you, we know that you are excited for Santa to come tonight. Sammy, your parents will be coming home safely to you in a few months. Mollie, we gave Santa a hint, and we think that you will love your gift. Meghan, it was hard to figure out what you would like, but we gave Santa a good clue. You will not see us during the year, but we will watch over you. Please study hard and work hard, like we do at the North Pole, and make a new house next year so we can come back.

Love always,
Your Elves

"What do you think they told Santa to bring?" asked Mom.

"Santa can't bring Sammy's parents," I said. "And I'm just too sad to think about presents."

Luckily, with all the last minute errands we had for Christmas day, no one had much time to think about the elves or presents.

Our traditional Christmas Eve dinner was steak and waffles. As the syrup from the waffles spread over to the steak, it made the best taste ever, sweet and savory. When we finished, we went to church. A few pews ahead of us sat Sammy and her grandparents.

"I bet she's praying her parents will have a safe return," I said. "I am, too."

When we got home, Mollie and I set out the milk and cookies for Santa. Mom handed us each a present.

"You can open this one now," she said.

We found a new pair of matching Christmas pajamas. Then Dad handed Mom a present, and she got the same pajamas!

When we finally kissed Mom and Dad good night, I asked, "Do you think the elves will be safe? Will they come back next year?"

"Just believe, Meghan," Mom said, kissing my forehead. "Just believe."

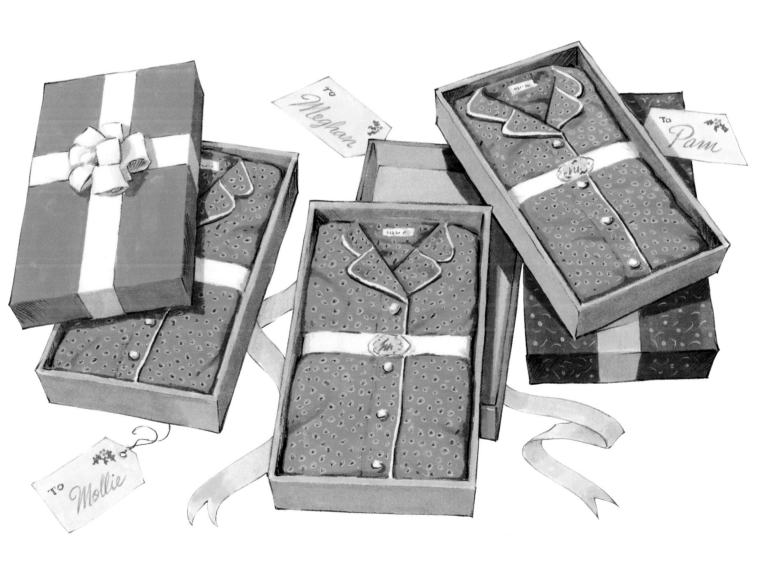

As soon as the grandfather clock struck seven, Mollie and I jumped on Mom and Dad's bed.

"We know he came! We saw our stockings!" Mollie shouted.

As soon as Mom and Dad could put on their robes, we sat on the landing and opened our stockings. We found candy canes, a little windup car, a yo-yo and some other small gifts. After the stockings, Dad always went down first so he'd be ready with the video.

"OK," Dad called up the stairs. "You can come down now."

We flew down. By the time we entered the family room, Mollie was already playing with a great big red barn and lots of horses.

I gently touched a piano keyboard. In my excitement about the elves, I had completely forgotten that I had been asking for piano lessons all fall. And, of course, there were notes.

Dear Meghan,

A tiny little Elf told me that you liked music as much as he does. He said you would really like to learn to play the piano. I hope you like the keyboard and that you will be able to start your music lessons.

Love, Santa

Dear Mollie,

A tiny Elf told me how much you love horses. She loves horses, too.

Love, Santa

We spent the rest of that happy day opening presents and preparing for Christmas dinner. Sammy and her grandparents were joining us.

We waited at the window until they pulled up.

When Sammy opened the car door, she was holding something.

"It's a puppy!" said Mollie. We darted out to greet them.

"Look what Santa brought me," Sammy cried. A little blond puppy wiggled in her arms.

I rubbed its fuzzy head. "What's its name?"

"Hans," she said. "I got a note from Santa, and I am sure Hans told him that I needed a puppy." She held out the note.

Dear Sammy,

I have heard from a very special Elf, that your parents have been deployed and you are living with your grandparents. He said you need a special friend. Although I usually do not give puppies for Christmas, your situation is different, so I will make an exception. I know you will make me proud and take very good care of this little guy.

Love Santa

After dinner, when I cleared my plate, I whispered to Mom, "I'm not even jealous. Sammy needs a puppy more than Mollie and I do. We have each other."

"What did I always say?" Mom whispered back to me. "Just believe."

The summer after that magical Christmas, Sammy's parents came home, and she moved back to Texas. We missed her, but we knew she was much happier. One day, as I practiced on the keyboard and Mollie played with her horses, Mom came in with a letter.

"It looks like it's from Sammy," she said.

In it was a picture of Sammy, her parents, and an almost full grown Hans. She looked so happy and proud.

Dear Meghan and Mollie,

I am so happy to be home with my mom and dad! Hans has grown up so much and has learned a lot of new tricks. He is my best friend! Mom and Dad told me we are going to go visit my grandparents next month. I can't wait to see you. You can meet my parents and play with Hans! Do you think it's too early to make a new gingerbread house?!

Love,
Sammy

bright sky press
HOUSTON, TEXAS

2365 Rice Blvd., Suite 202
Houston, Texas 77005

ISBN: 978-1-931721-10-3

10   9   8   7   6   5   4   3   2   1

Library of Congress Cataloging-in-Publication Data on file with publisher.

Editorial Direction: Lucy Herring Chambers
Designer: Marla Y. Garcia

Printed in Canada through Friesens